WELCOME TO THE WORLD

Geronimo Stilton

Published by Sweet Cherry Publishing Limited
Unit 36, Vulcan House,
Vulcan Road,
Leicester, LE5 3EF
United Kingdom

First published in the UK in 2021
2021 edition

2 4 6 8 10 9 7 5 3 1

ISBN: 978-1-78226-800-0

Text by Geronimo Stilton
Art Director: Iacopo Bruno
Graphic Designer: Laura Dal Maso / theWorldofDOT
Original cover illustration by Roberto Ronchi (design) and Alessandro Muscillo (colour)
Illustrations by Roberto Ronchi (drawing) Christian Aliprandi and Davide Turotti (colour).
Artistic coordination with Gògo Gó, and artistic assistance by Laura Martinelli.
Initial and final page illustrations by Roberto Ronchi and Ennio Bufi MAD5, Studio Parlapà and
Andrea Cavallini. Map illustrations by Andrea Da Rold and Andrea Cavallini
Cover layout and typography by Dominika Plocka
Interior layout and typography by Matthew Ellero
Graphics by Merenguita Gingermouse and Michela Battaglin
© 2005 – 2018 Mondadori Libri S.p.A. for PIEMME, Italia
© 2021 UK edition, Sweet Cherry Publishing
International Rights © Atlantyca S.p.A. – via Leopardi 8, 20123 Milano, Italy
Translation © 2006 by Edizioni Piemme S.p.A.

Original title: La Mummia Senza Nome
Based on an original idea by Elisabetta Dami

www.geronimostilton.com/uk

Stilton is the name of a famous English cheese. It is a registered trademark of the Stilton Cheese Makers'
Association. For more information go to www.stiltoncheese.com

www.sweetcherrypublishing.com

Printed and bound in Turkey
T.OP005

Geronimo Stilton

THE MUMMY WITH NO NAME

Sweet Cherry

It Was a Cold October Afternoon ...

It was a **COld** October afternoon. Outside, the wind whipped the leaves around in swirls of red and gold. I was glad I wasn't a field mouse. I'd be **FREEZING** my tail off! Luckily, I was nice and warm, snuggled inside my **comfy** home doing one of my favourite things ... reading.

I was lazily reading a book ...

... sipping a cup of hot cocoa ...

... munching on cheese puffs ...

... when my mobile phone rang.

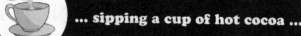

I received a text message:

> STILTON, I NEED YOUR HELP ON
> A MYSTERIOUS CASE.
> SIGNED PROFESSOR CYRIL
> B. SANDSNOUT

Do you know **Professor Sandsnout?** He is an expert on everything there is to know about **EGYPT**. He is also the director of the Egyptian Mouseum in New Mouse City. And he is one of my dearest friends.

Oops! I think I forgot to introduce myself. Silly me! My name is Stilton, **GERONIMO STILTON**.

W-w-who Are
Y-y-you?

I wondered why Professor Sandsnout needed my help. I decided to go visit him at the MOUSEUM and find out. Of course, a trip to the mouseum is always a lot more **fun** with my favourite little nephew, Benjamin.

I quickly called my Aunt Sweetfur's mouse hole. That's where Benjamin lives.

"Would you like to come with me to the **EGYPTIAN MOUSEUM?**" I asked my nephew. "You can bring a friend if you'd like."

There was an excited squeak on the other end of the phone.

I took off for Aunt Sweetfur's right away. I knocked on the front door, then strolled inside. That's when I was hit with a big surprise. And I mean **HIT**.

9

GERONIMO

STILTON

With a **WHOOSH**, the kitchen door crashed open and slammed me right in the whiskers!

"Aaaah!" I screeched before I passed out.

As soon as I came round, I saw a little female mouse standing over me. She had black hair that she wore in lots of tiny braids. A green bandana with little hearts on it covered the top of her head. And an **EXPENSIVE** camera hung around her neck.

She grabbed my paw and squeezed it hard. **HOLEY CHEESE!** Who taught this mouse how to shake paws? **MAD MOUSE MAX**, the bone-crushing rodent wrestler? I wondered if I'd ever be able to write again.

"W-w-who are y-y-you?" I stammered, massaging my sore paw. The strange little mouse broke into a wide grin. "I'm **Bugsy Wugsy!** That's **B-U-G-S-Y W-U-G-S-Y!**" she shrieked. My ear started ringing. I wondered if I'd ever hear out of it again. First my paw, then my ear. Who was this mouselet, and what would she do next? **I was afraid to find out.**

BUGSY WUGSY

FIRST NAME: Bugsy

LAST NAME: Wugsy

NICKNAME: Little Tornado

WHO SHE IS: Petunia Pretty Paws's niece

HER INTERESTS: Like her aunt Petunia, she loves everything about nature, animals, and plants

HER FAVOURITE SPORT: Climbing trees

HER SECRET: She has a crush on Benjamin!

Bugsy Wugsy

May I Call You Uncle G?

I stared at Bugsy. Now the little mouse was jumping around like Benjamin's robotic rat doll on **SUPER-HIGH** speed.

"I can't believe it's really you – Geronimo Stilton! I've heard so much about you! You're the publisher of *The Rodent's Gazette*, the most famouse newspaper in New Mouse City!" she squeaked. "May I call you Uncle Geronimo? Or how about ... **Uncle G?**"

She began skipping around me faster and faster. I was getting dizzy just looking at her. Then there was a sickening **CRUNCH**.

"Yikes! My tail!" I screamed at the top of my lungs.

Bugsy stopped skipping. "**OOPS**, sorry, Uncle G," she said. She grabbed a chair.

"Here, why don't you sit down?" she suggested. But while she was helping me into the chair, she accidentally stomped on my paw. **"Yikes! My paw!"** I screamed again.

Bugsy shook her head. "Excuse me, Uncle G," she squeaked. "But you really should be a little more **CAREFUL**. At this rate, you're going to end up in the emergency room. How do you even manage to get through the day?"

I was fuming. Who did this **LITTLE PIPSQUEAK** think she was?

Luckily, Aunt Sweetfur rushed over before I pulled out all of my fur. "Poor Geronimo," she gushed. In a flash, she bandaged my tail. Then she massaged my paw and made us each a cup of steaming **hot chocolate**.

"So, Benjamin told me that you are going to have a **HALLOWEEN** party," Aunt Sweetfur said, sitting down next to me.

I nodded. I'm not really big on Halloween — it's such a **SPOOKY** holiday. But I love throwing theme parties.

Just then, Bugsy screeched so loudly I felt like I'd been standing in the front row of a **FUZZY FUZZBORN** concert for twelve hours.

15

"A **P-A-R-T-Y?** Yeeeeeah! I love parties!" she squeaked.

The little mouse flung her paws around me in a **CRUSHING HUG**.

"Can't breathe ... can't breathe," I gasped.

"What's that, Uncle G? Did you say you can't wait?" she yelped. "Oh, I can't wait for the party, either!"

I rolled my eyes. Well, Bugsy was right about one thing. I couldn't wait. **That is, I couldn't wait to get away from Bugsy!**

AH, PETUNIA

Right at that moment, my mobile phone **RANG**.

"Hello. This is Stilton, *Geronimo Stilton*," I said.

A sweet voice answered on the other end. "Hi, G!" it squeaked.

I immediately blushed. Thank goodness, the caller couldn't see me! It was my fascinating friend **Petunia Pretty Paws**. She's a TV reporter who has dedicated her life to saving animals and nature. I have had a huge crush on her for the longest time. But whenever I'm around her I turn into a babbling, blundering fool!

"I just wanted to check on my **favourite** niece," Petunia squeaked into the phone.

Y-y-your niece?

I didn't know what she was talking about. "**Y-y-your niece?**" I muttered, confused.

Just then, Bugsy pulled at my jacket sleeve. "Is that Aunt Petunia?" she asked.

My head was **SPINNING**. I couldn't believe it. How could such a quiet, gentle, sweet mouse like Petunia have such a hyper, loud, **annoying** niece like Bugsy?

"Yes, Bugsy is my niece," Petunia was saying into the phone. "And I need you to do me a favour and take good care of her for a week while I'm away. Thanks, G. Bye-bye!"

I hung up the phone in a **daze**. Responsible for Bugsy? I wasn't thrilled about that, but I'd do anything for Petunia.

"Hey, Uncle G, why are you smiling like that? Are you in love with my aunt? Will you marry her? Can I be your flower mouse? What kind of wedding cake are you going to have? Ooh, I have an idea! I'll call Aunt Petunia and tell her you're **in love** with her," Bugsy squeaked.

I jumped to my paws. **"NO! NO! DONT CALL PETUNIA!"** I shouted.

Bugsy shook her head. "Face it, Uncle G, you're one **LOVESICK MOUSE!**" she insisted.

My head began to pound. I felt like I was going to explode. "I am not your uncle! I am not sick!" I yelled.

Just then, the phone rang. It was Petunia Pretty Paws again.

"G? I want to remind you to treat my niece well," she said. "She's such an angel." I shook my head as if in a trance. Then I hung up the phone with a deep sigh. What was it about Petunia that made me all **weak in the paws?**

I caught Bugsy watching me. She had a smirk on her snout as she turned to Benjamin. "Do you know that when your uncle talks with my aunt, he really looks very **goofy**," she told my nephew.

I pretended not to hear. **What else could I do?**

D-D-DON'T
BE AFRAID!

Waving goodbye to Aunt Sweetfur, Benjamin, Bugsy, and I headed out to the Egyptian Mouseum. When we got there, I looked around. How **STRANGE**. Usually there is a **LOOOOOOOOOOONG** line to get in to the mouseum. But today, there wasn't a rodent in sight.

I pulled open the heavy door. It let out a loud **CREAK** that made me jump. I don't know why, but something about the empty mouseum gave me the creeps. In the

THE GODDESS BASTET

With the body of a woman and the head of a cat, this ancient Egyptian goddess was the protector of fire, cats, pregnant women, and the home. To obtain her favours, the ancient Egyptians offered fresh fish to house cats, which were considered to be her earthly representatives. Her temple was located in the ancient city of Bubastis in northern Egypt.

Great Hall, we were greeted by an enormouse statue of Bastet, the Egyptian goddess with the head of a cat. **CHEESE NIBLETS**, that cat made me **SHIVER**! I grabbed Benjamin's and Bugsy's paws.

"D-d-don't worry, everything is OK. D-d-don't be afraid," I stammered.

Benjamin **SQUEEZED** my paw. "I'm not afraid, Uncle Geronimo," he squeaked.

"Don't worry about us, Uncle G! We're not afraid of anything!" Bugsy yelled at the top of her lungs. Her voice echoed in the deserted mouseum.

Right then, Bugsy realised that she had forgotten her camera in the car.

"We'll be right back, Uncle G. You wait for us here," she hollered. She grabbed Benjamin's paw and sprinted back outside.

I stood alone in the cold, dusty lobby.

"Achoo!" I sneezed. Did I mention I'm allergic to dust and mould and even rubber flip-flops? But that's another story.

Anyway, where was I? Oh yes, I was standing alone in the dark Great Hall of the mouseum when I heard a loud **BANG**.

I spun around. The velvet rope that surrounded an ancient stone coffin known as a sarcophagus had collapsed in a heap. **HOW STRANGE.**

I went closer to read the plaque in front of the coffin: THE MVMMY WITH NO NAME. I sniffed the air. What was that disgusting musty smell?

All of a sudden, a real MVMMY, covered in dust and wrapped in yellowed bandages, emerged from the sarcophagus. I froze. **RAT-MUNCHING RATTLESNAKES!**

"I am the Mummy with No Name!" the mummy roared. I was so scared I lost my squeak.

The Mummy with No Name shuffled **CLOSER**. It almost touched my whiskers.

"Leave, before it is too late!" it hissed in my ear. Then it stumbled down the dark corridor, leaving a trail of thousand-year-old dust behind it.

I couldn't move. I couldn't breathe. I couldn't see. A sudden **FLASH** of light blinded me. Then a voice shouted, "Hey, Uncle G! Hope you don't mind my taking your picture. You know, you really should trim your **whiskers**. They're a mess."

Bugsy and Benjamin were back. **But had they seen the mummy?**

I'M NOT CRAZY!

I was a wreck. My paws were shaking. My whiskers were twitching. And my eyes felt like they were about to pop out of their sockets, roll back to my car, and drive away without me!

"I-s-s-s-saw a m-m-m-mummy! But D-d-don't be a-f-f-fraid!" I managed to stutter.

Benjamin looked **SURPRISED**. "A mummy?" he murmured.

"Y-yes, a real mummy. And he told me to leave b-b-before it's too late," I added.

Benjamin looked around. "I don't see anyone. Are you sure you're **feeling OK**, Uncle Geronimo?" he squeaked.

Bugsy looked at me. Then she began to whisper in Benjamin's ear.

I couldn't hear everything she said, but I did make out the words **looney tunes, nuts,** and **lost his cheddar**.

I puffed up my fur. "**I am not crazy!** I did see a mummy!" I insisted.

Bugsy giggled. "Well, of course you saw a mummy, Uncle G," she said. "There are loads of mummies here. We're in the **EGYPTIAN MOUSEUM!**"

I groaned. I was beginning to think I should head right on back to my cosy mouse hole when someone – or something – pinched my tail.

"RANCID RAT HAIRS!" I shrieked. "The mummy!"

Then I fainted.

When I came round, an INTELLECTUAL-LOOKING mouse with blondish fur and round eyeglasses was standing between Benjamin and Bugsy, leaning over me. "You're right, Geronimo. You did see a MVMMY. That's why I asked you to come to the mouseum. I need your help in solving the mystery," the rodent murmured.

I sat up immediately. I would recognise that mouse anywhere. **It was my dear old friend, Professor Cyril B. Sandsnout.**

PROFESSOR CYRIL B. SANDSNOUT

NAME: Cyril

LAST NAME: Sandsnout

NICKNAME: Desert Rat

WHO HE IS: Director of the Egyptian Mouseum in New Mouse City

HIS WORK: Travelling around the world in search of mysterious papyruses

HIS HOBBY: Reading joke books. He loves to tell jokes to his friends and relatives

HIS SECRET: He adores playing pranks!

Two New Assistants for the Professor

"Professor Sandsnout!" I squeaked.

The professor put one paw up in front of his snout.

"**Shhhhhhh!** Someone could be listening! Follow me!" he whispered.

The professor turned right, then left, then right, then left, then down a long hallway to a **round** room. He crossed the round room, then a **RECTANGULAR** room, and then a **SQUARE** room. Benjamin, Bugsy, and I followed close behind him. **HOLEY CHEESE!** This place was worse than the corn maze at Rascal Ralph's Festival Fun Farm in Scamperville!

At last, the professor stopped in front of a tiny door. A plaque on the door read:

Private Office
Professor Cyril B. Sandsnout
DO NOT ENTER

The professor pulled an **ENORMOUSE** key ring from his pocket. Then he selected a key and opened the door. We found ourselves in an office that was covered in dust. **"Achoo! Achoo!"** I sneezed.

After about three hundred more sneezes, I looked around. The place was covered from floor to ceiling with books. Do you know what all of the books were about? **ANCIENT EGYPT**, of course!

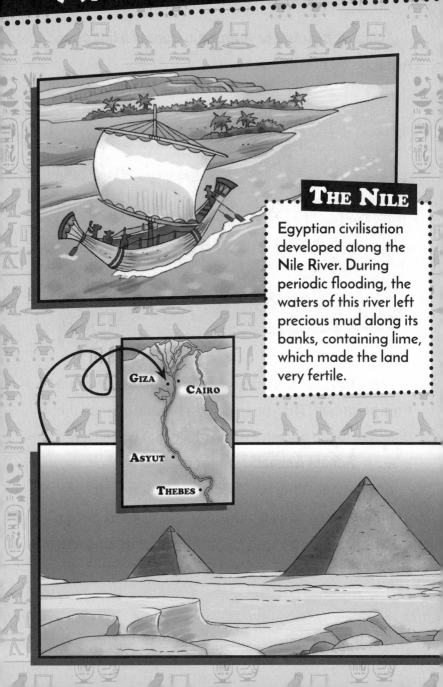

THE NILE

Egyptian civilisation developed along the Nile River. During periodic flooding, the waters of this river left precious mud along its banks, containing lime, which made the land very fertile.

GIZA

CAIRO

ASYUT

THEBES

THE PYRAMIDS OF GIZA

The plains of Giza are dominated by three pyramids, which were built by the pharaohs Khufu, Khafre, and Menkaure about 4,500 years ago. The Great Pyramid, built by Khufu, is approximately 147 metres tall, and the base is immense - each side is 230 metres long. It took more than twenty years to construct.

THE SPHINX

The Sphinx is 73 metres long and 20 metres tall. It may be the largest statue ever carved from a single block of limestone. Pharaoh Khafre had it sculpted (around 2620 BC). Thutmoses IV, who ruled from 1412 to 1402 BC, freed the Sphinx from the encroaching sand and gave it a face-lift. Legend blames Napoleon and his troops for shooting off the nose around 1798, but this story isn't true.

In Greek mythology, the Sphinx was a monster with the body of a lion and the head of a human. It lived near the city of Thebes. It would devour all those who, when passing through, did not know how to solve its extremely difficult riddles or enigmas.

The professor gave a deep sigh and turned to me. "This room is **SOUNDPROOF** from any eavesdroppers. Now we can talk without being heard, dear friend," he said, smiling.

I smiled back, but I must admit the whole soundproof room thing made me a little **panicky**. I mean, what if the door got stuck and we couldn't get out? No one would be able to hear our screams! We'd end up just like the mummies in this place – very **OLD** and very **dead**. Well, except for the one I saw walking around. I shivered. I introduced Professor Sandsnout to Benjamin and Bugsy to take my mind off things.

The professor talked to the **LITTLE MICE** about mummies, sarcophagi, and Pyramids.

Then he made them his official assistants.

THE MYSTERY
OF THE MUMMY
WITH NO NAME

Once Benjamin and Bugsy had stopped **SQUEAKING** over their new positions, the professor turned serious.

"Now that you are here," he began. "I'm hoping you can help me solve a **mystery**. As you can see, the **EGYPTIAN MOUSEUM** is deserted. That's because something is scaring the visitors away!"

I chewed my whiskers. "**THE M–M–M–MUMMY WITH NO N–N–N–NAME?**" I stammered.

Professor Sandsnout nodded. He explained how he had been doing some work down in the mouseum's basement the week before. Apparently, the area had been closed for many years. But the professor found a **GOLDEN SARCOPHAGUS** there. It contained

a **STRANGE** mummy that the professor called The Mummy with No Name. He put the sarcophagus in the Great Hall, so all of the visitors could see it.

"That's right where I saw it," I murmured.

The professor nodded, and explained how the mysterious mummy had been **TERRORISING** visitors ever since. "It warns everyone to stay away. Then it disappears in a cloud of dust," he said.

My fur stood on end. **I had seen The Mummy with No Name!**

I AM THE MUMMY WITH NO NAME!

A mysterious mummy ...

... who howls threats ...

... and disappears ...

... in a cloud of dust!

I Am the Pharaoh ...

Professor Sandsnout continued, "On the inside of the **GOLDEN SARCOPHAGUS**, there was also an ancient manuscript written on **PAPYRUS**. I'll show it to you now. Unfortunately, the ending is missing."

HIEROGLYPHICS

The word hieroglyphics means "sacred incision." It comes from the Greek words hieros (sacred) and glyphein (incision). There are two types of hieroglyphics: ideograms, or drawings that represent concepts (for example, the sun was shown as a disk), and phonograms, or drawings that represent sounds. In ancient Egypt, only scribes knew how to write in hieroglyphics. That is why scribes were held in high esteem.

Scribe

The papyrus found by Professor Sandsnout in the golden sarcophagus of The Mummy with No Name.

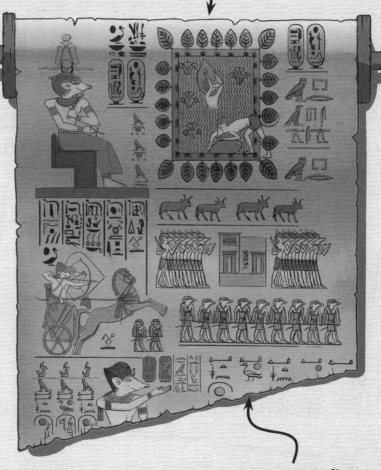

Unfortunately, the papyrus is missing the end piece.

Professor Sandsnout took out his wallet and pulled a piece of yellowed paper from it. Then he read these words out loud.

I am the pharaoh of Upper and Lower Egypt. I am now resting in a priceless golden sarcophagus. I ruled over the fertile lands near the River Nile and all of the rodents who lived there. I lived in a large palace with many servants. I commanded a powerful army. I knew many riches in my life. But my most precious treasure was ...

Here the professor stopped and sighed. "As you can see ... the **PAPYRUS** is torn," he said, holding up the paper. "Now we can only guess what the **precious treasure** might be or where it is. **Oh, if only we could find that missing piece of papyrus.**"

A treasure ...

WHO TURNED OFF THE LIGHTS?

Before anyone could respond, we heard a sound – **C**R**E**A**K**! I nearly jumped right out of my fur.

"W-w-what was that?" I gasped. My heart was beating so hard I felt like I had just finished the New Mouse City Marathon. Of course, the closest I'd ever got to the marathon was the time I watched it on TV while eating a giant double-decker cheddar sandwich. **Yum!**

BRR ...

For a minute, I almost forgot about the mummy. But then, we heard another **C**R**E**A**K**. And then another, and another. Suddenly, all the lights went out.

44

"Stop! Who's there? Who turned off the lights?" Professor Sandsnout yelled.

The same **disgusting** musty odor I had smelled earlier filled the air. Then we heard **someone** – or **SOMETHING** – moaning.

WooooooooOOOOOOOo!

GOOOO AWAAAAAAY...

... OR YOU'LL BEEEEEEEEE...

... SOOOOOOOOOOORRY!

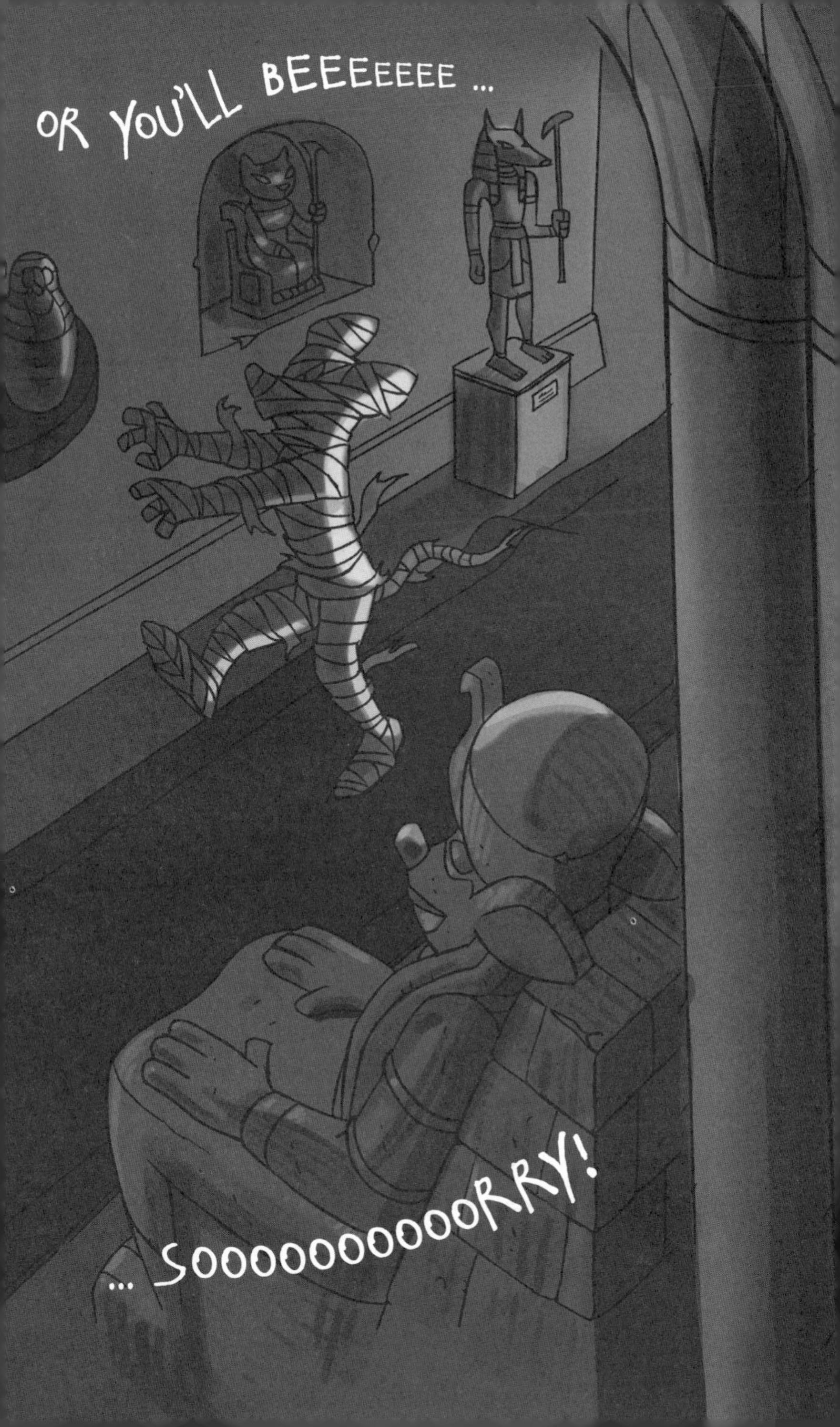
OR YOU'LL BEEEEEEE ...
... SOOOOOOOOOORRY!

A swishing sound followed. It sounded as if someone with bandaged feet was coming toward us. They shuffled closer and closer. Was it the mummy? Or some other creepy Egyptian monster? **RAT-MUNCHING RATTLESNAKES!** How much more could one mouse take?

Just when I was certain I would die of fright, we heard a muffled little laugh.

"HEE, HEE, HEE, HEE ..." it cackled. The laugh grew weaker and weaker and weaker until it was **gone**.

Who was laughing at us?

Professor Sandsnout scrambled around in the dark and came back with a torch. The beam of light threw **EERIE** shadows around the room. Then he headed toward the circuit breaker and turned on the lights.

I looked around. Everything looked the same as before. Except for one thing – the papyrus was gone!

The professor's fur turned as white as a slice of **mozzarella**. He searched the floor, his desk, the inside of his waste bin. But the papyrus was nowhere to be found. Someone had stolen it.

A MYSTERIOUS SHADOW

The professor looked **glum**. "Oh, why did I let that **PAPYRUS** out of my paws? Now we've got to find both parts," he groaned.

We started down the long, long hallway. I lagged behind. All of the dust was turning me into a sneezing machine. **"Achoo!"** I squeaked again and again. Finally, I stopped. And that's when I saw it. A **MYSTERIOUS SHADOW** was growing on the wall.

It grew **BIGGER**. And **BIGGER**. Who was following me?

The shadow stretched toward me like a claw! I tried to **scream**, but no sound came out. Instead, I heard another sound. The sound of someone singing in an old, raspy voice.

"Mummies creeping here and there.

Mummies, mummies everywhere!

They stink of mould and rotten things.

They'll make you wish you had some wings.

Mummies hiding, watching, waiting,

Making you sweat, anticipating ...

Mummies!"

The shadow was creeping closer and closer. "**PLEASE, DON'T HURT ME!** I come in peace!" I yelped. I held my breath as I turned the corner.

But there was no mummy there at all. The shadow belonged to an **old lady mouse** with thick glasses. She was washing the mouseum floor with a bucket of soapy water and a mop. When she smiled, I could see she was wearing dentures.

I turned purple with **embarrassment**. So this was who had scared me out of my wits? This frail little old lady mouse who looked like she wouldn't swat a fly? I gave her a sheepish smile. Then I **RAN OFF**.

Soon I **CAUGHT UP** with Benjamin, Bugsy, and the professor. Professor Sandsnout gave me a sheet of paper. "This is the floor plan of the mouseum, Geronimo," he explained. **"You will need it to help me search for the missing papyrus."**

Mummies creeping here and there.

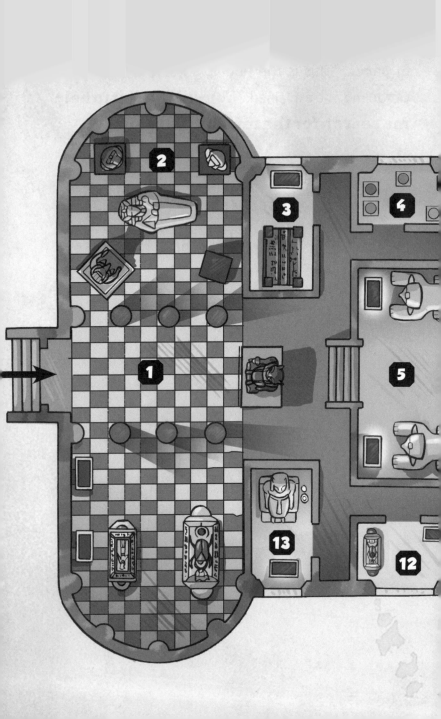

THE HALL
OF SCARABS

After a little while, we reached what was known as the **HALL OF SCARABS**. We tried to go inside, but the door was locked. Professor Sandsnout turned back to get the keys from his office.

Benjamin and Bugsy played word games while they waited. I would have joined in, but I was too busy sneezing. *"Achoo! Achoo! Achoo!"*

"God bless you!" a little voice called out. It seemed to be coming from a dark corner at the end of the hall.

"Thank you!" I answered automatically. Then I froze. **Yikes!** Was it the MVMMY?

A minute later, the same voice began to moan, "Wooo! Go Awaaaay! or You'll be sorrrrrry!"

I was about to run away with my tail between my legs. But Bugsy and Benjamin were **RUNNING** toward the dark corner! How **DARING**. How **BRAVE**. How **NUTS**.

Bugsy waved her camera in the air. "Hey, Mummy, do you like having your **picture** taken?" she yelled. Just then, the mummy raised a billowing cloud of **DUST**.

Now everybody was sneezing!

I want to take a picture of the mummy!

ACHOO! ACHOO! Achoo! Achoo! Achoo! Achoo! ACHOO! ACHOO! Achoo! ACHOO! ACHOO! Achoo!

The mummy took advantage of our *SNEEZING* fits and ran off down the hall. At that moment, Professor Sandsnout came back with the keys. We quickly told him what had happened.

"The MUMMY appeared again? Incredible ..." he squeaked, unlocking the door.

We entered the Hall of Scarabs.

A beautiful collection of **gold**, **silver**, **copper**, **jade**, **alabaster**, **ruby**, **emerald**, and **topaz** Egyptian beetles was on exhibit. The professor explained that the scarab was a sacred symbol to the ancient Egyptians. It was the symbol of immortality.

A *shiver* ran up my spine. **BUGS** make my fur crawl.

"D-d-don't be afraid," I told Benjamin and Bugsy, grabbing their paws.

"I'm not afraid!" Benjamin replied.

"Don't you just love bugs, Uncle G?" Bugsy said, grinning.

THE HALL OF SARCOPHAGI

While the others were **ADMIRING** the beetles, I stepped into the next room to get as far away from the bugs as I could. The room was called the **HALL OF SARCOPHAGI**. In it, a long row of sarcophagi leaned against one wall. The coffins were made of marble, granite, and painted wood. There were even some made of **GOLD!**

Many of the sarcophagi had faces painted on them. I guessed that these were the faces of the dead mice inside. **CHEESE NIBLETS!** Being around all of those dead mice was beginning to make me feel queasy. Then I spotted one sarcophagus that was empty.

I bent down to read its plaque, when ... someone behind me pushed me inside! The lid closed on top of me with a sickening **THUD**. I was trapped!

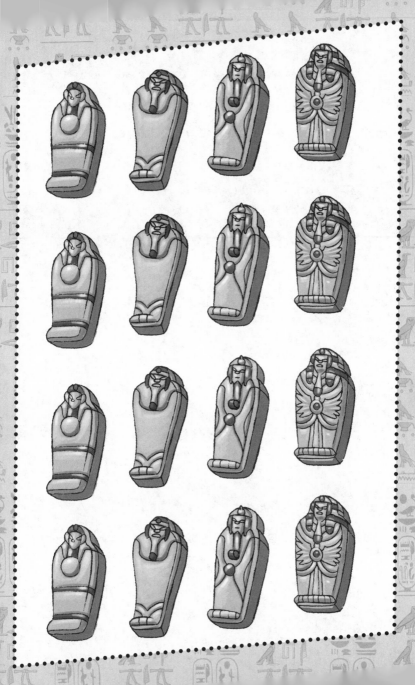

"Help!!!" I screamed at the top of my lungs. Mouldy mozzarella! I was terrified beyond belief.

Oh, how did I get myself into this mess?

Tears rolled down my fur.

Luckily, my friends had heard my shouts. The lid opened and they quickly pulled me out of the coffin.

"Were you **CRYING**, Uncle G?" Bugsy asked.

"Um, er, no. I just got some dust in my eye," I lied.

After all, I didn't want everyone thinking I was a 'fraidy mouse.

THE HIDDEN
TRAPDOOR

After a lot of work, we finished searching the whole Egyptian Mouseum. But we didn't find the missing **PAPYRUS** or the treasure. Luckily, Professor Sandsnout had a plan.

"Let's go back to the **UNDERGROUND CHAMBER** where I found The Mummy with No Name. Maybe we'll find something there," he suggested.

Oh no, I thought. Not the basement. I hate basements. They're so dark and cold. And some are **CRAWLING** with bugs. Did I tell you I hate bugs?

I bit my lip and followed the others with shaky paws. The professor led the way down the old spiral staircase. The flickering candle he held in his paw made **SPOOKY SHADOWS** on the walls.

DOWN, **DOWN**, **DOWN** we went until we reached the underground chamber. I looked around. The place was packed with stuff, just like the professor had said – urns, chests, bowls, statues. And everything was covered in dust. What a **PIGSTY!** Didn't any mouse ever clean up around here? This place was almost as bad as **PACKRAT PETE'S** living room. That rodent never threw anything away. Professor Sandsnout put the candle on the floor. "This is where I found the golden sarcophagus that held The Mummy with No Name," he explained.

There was so much dust I could hardly breathe. I began to **PANIC**. What if I was having a life-threatening asthma attack? Then I remembered I don't have asthma. What a relief! I relaxed. I stared at the dusty floor. That's when I noticed some **STRANGE FOOTPRINTS**. I pointed them out to the professor, and we decided to follow them. The footprints led to a trapdoor on the floor.

The professor grabbed the heavy metal ring on the door and pulled with all of his might. **"Heeeave-ho!"**

he squeaked. The door popped open. I was impressed. Who knew Professor Sandsnout had such **STRONG MUSCLES?**

A Very Dark Mousetrap

We all peered down into the hole. "It's a **SECRET CHAMBER!**" the professor exclaimed. "Let's go down and check it out."

I began twisting my tail up in knots. **Oh, how did I get myself into these scary fur-raising situations?**

One by one, we clambered down into the chamber. It was as dark as my mouse hole at midnight. Just then, a gust of wind blew out our candle and a loud **THUMP** echoed all around us. Everyone gasped. That thump could only mean one thing.

Someone – or **SOMETHING** – had just shut the trapdoor on us.

70

At that moment, we heard the mummy's raspy voice moaning. "Youuuu WIIIILLLL NEVVVVER GEt ooooooUUUUUt!" it cried.

My tummy flip-flopped. "Professor, please tell me there's another exit," I pleaded.

In the dark, Professor Sandsnout sighed. "No, there isn't. We have about an hour of air. Let's try hard to breathe slowly and not to move around. That way, we can conserve the oxygen," he suggested.

I went into full **PANIC** mode. My fur began to drip with sweat. My paws shook. My whiskers twitched uncontrollably. **"Waaaa!!!"** I shrieked like a newborn mouselet.

"Geronimo, don't get excited. You're using up the oxygen!" the professor scolded.

"Yeah, Uncle G, keep your fur on!" Bugsy added.

I clamped a paw over my mouth. We were trapped in a **GIANT TOMB!** I tried to remember one of the relaxing exercises I had learned from my yoga teacher, Penny Pretzel Paws.

72

Before I could figure it out, an idea **POPPED** into my head. I told the professor to get on my shoulders. Then I told Benjamin to climb on top of the professor's shoulders. Finally, I told Bugsy to get on Benjamin's shoulders. **CHEESECAKE!** My idea worked! We had formed our very own rodent ladder.

Once Bugsy was at the **TOP**, she was able to push the trapdoor open.

CHEESE NIBLETS! My friends weighed a lot! Bugsy scampered out. Then she came back with a rope. One by one, she helped to pull us out of the dark underground chamber. I was so glad to be free that I started **BAWLING** again. Everyone stared at me. I turned bright red.

Here's the trapdoor!

Hurry up!

Come on!

Ow!

Luckily, a strange **SWISHING** sound took the attention off of me. Someone was hiding in the darkness. I turned around just in time to spot her. It was the little old **cleaning lady!** She had the strangest look on her snout. "Nice weather we're having," she said. That's when I noticed something sticking out of her purse.

It was the rolled **PAPYRUS!** My eyes nearly popped out of my fur.

"Madam, give us back the papyrus!" I squeaked.

"Papyrus? What papyrus?" the old lady mumbled.

Then she took off like a shot. I was amazed. She was kicking up her paws like an Olympic track rat! She raced toward the stairs, snickering, and leaving only a **CLOUD OF DUST** behind her.

I KNOW WHO YOU ARE!

Bugsy and Benjamin **sprang** into action. First, Bugsy grabbed the papyrus with one paw. Then she reached for the old lady's hair. The little old lady was wearing a **WIG!** Her real hair was long and blonde. Then Benjamin reached for her dress. Under it, the mouse wore a **SLEEK BLACK JUMPSUIT.** With a snort, she whipped off false teeth and a rubber mask. **HOLEY CHEESE!**

"I know who you are!" I squeaked. "You're **THE SHADOW!**" Everyone in New Mouse City had heard of the Shadow. She was a notorious thief who was known for her clever disguises.

"That's right, mousey. I am the Shadow," she boasted.

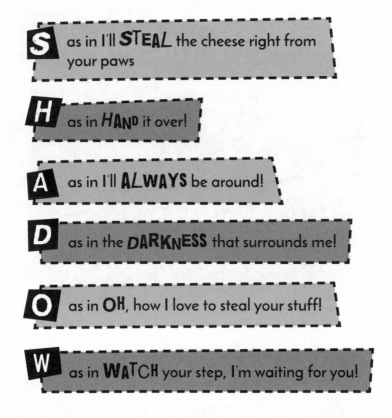

S as in **STEAL** the cheese right from your paws

H as in **HAND** it over!

A as in I'll **ALWAYS** be around!

D as in the **DARKNESS** that surrounds me!

O as in **OH**, how I love to steal your stuff!

W as in **WATCH** your step, I'm waiting for you!

"So you were the cleaning lady and the mummy!" I exclaimed. "You wanted to **SCARE** everyone away from the mouseum so you could find the mummy's **TREASURE**."

The Shadow smiled.

THE SHADOW

The Shadow is Sally Ratmousen's mysterious cousin. (Sally is the owner of The Daily Rat and is Geronimo's number-one rival.) The Shadow is a fascinating rodent who is willing to do anything to get rich. A master of disguises, she knows all the tricks so she can go about without being recognised.

But before I could say anything else, the Shadow began spraying something into the air.

PUTRID CHEESE PUFFS! She was spraying us with a cloud of dust so thick that even my supersonic cheese slicer wouldn't be able to cut through it! We all began **SNEEZING** uncontrollably.

As soon as the dust settled, I looked around. The Shadow had **DISAPPEARED**.

"She got away again," I said, sighing, feeling down in the dumps. We had been searching so hard for the mummy's treasure. But we still came up **empty-pawed**.

Just then, Benjamin began tugging on my sleeve. I looked down and saw that he was holding a **YELLOW SHEET OF PAPER**. "What's this, Uncle Geronimo? Bugsy and I found it under a big wooden chest when we were trapped underground," he squeaked.

I looked at the paper. I cleaned my glasses. I looked at the paper again. It couldn't be! But it was! **Benjamin and Bugsy had found the missing piece of the papyrus!**

THE PHARAOH'S TREASURE

Here's the first fragment of the papyrus!

Here's the missing fragment!

Professor Sandsnout was **ECSTATIC**. He hugged Benjamin and Bugsy. "Great work, you two! Now we can finally figure out what the pharaoh's **PRECIOUS TREASURE** is!" he cried excitedly.

We went back to the professor's office. We were all curious to find out what the treasure would be. Would it be **GOLD?** Would it be **jewels?** Carefully, the professor fit the two pieces of **PAPYRUS** together. Then he began to translate the mysterious Egyptian hieroglyphics ...

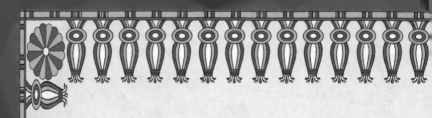

I am the pharaoh of Upper
and Lower Egypt.

I am now resting in a priceless
golden sarcophagus.

I ruled over the fertile lands near
the River Nile and all of the rodents
who lived there.

I lived in a large palace with
many servants.

I commanded a powerful army.

I knew many riches in my life.

But my most precious treasure was
my beloved, loving bride, Neferati.

Beautiful and wise was Neferati,
She squeaked into my life
Just when I needed her most.

Her voice was like music to my ears.
Her smile was like the brightest star
in the sky.

The love that united us
Was truly worth more than gold.

Therefore, my heart's desire
Is to always rest
At the side of my beloved bride.
We were close in life,
and so shall be in death ...

This is the desire of
Pharaoh Akhenraten.

When Professor Sandsnout finished translating, no one squeaked a word. What a wonderful **love story**. Maybe someday I would be head-over-paws in love, just like the pharaoh.

The professor turned on the computer. "Let's see what we can find out about Pharaoh Akhenraten," he said. He typed in the name. **"Here it is!"** he exclaimed. He began to read out loud. "Pharaoh Akhenraten was married to the beautiful, wise, and extremely talkative **Neferati**. It is said their love was stronger than the sharpest cheddar. They had twelve children. Their rule was happy and long. The pharaoh was against battles and war. He strove to bring **peace, love,** and **happiness** to all of his people."

The pharaoh Akhenraten and his beloved bride, Neferati, and their twelve children!

Benjamin grabbed my paw. "If the pharaoh wished so much to be buried next to Neferati, then can we find a way to **reunite** them, Uncle?" he asked.

Professor Sandsnout stared at the computer, deep in thought. He tugged on his beard, gnawed his paw nails, then twisted his tail up in a knot. Finally, he jumped out of his seat and pumped one paw in the air. **"Yes, we can do it!" he squeaked.**

We can do it!

85

A LOVE THAT WILL
LAST FOREVER

The professor contacted the Minister of Culture of New Mouse City. He got permission to take the mummy of Akhenraten back to **CAIRO**, the capital of Egypt.

Since we helped find the missing papyrus, Professor Sandsnout asked **all of us** to join him. Even my friend Petunia Pretty Paws was allowed to come along.

It was a long trip, but at last we arrived at the Cairo Mouseum.

Akhenraten's sarcophagus was taken to the **HALL OF MUMMIES**. It was placed next to Queen Neferati.

As the mummies were brought together, Professor Sandsnout spoke in a **SOLEMN** voice.

"O kindhearted Akhenraten," he squeaked. "We have returned you to Egypt, the land where you were born, and placed you beside your beloved bride. May the two of you sleep peacefully for all eternity."

I **smiled**. It was a great feeling to know that we had made the pharaoh's last wish come true. Beside me,

Here are the sarcophagi of Akhenraten and Neferati ... finally together !

Petunia Pretty Paws sighed. "How romantic." She beamed, grabbing my paw.

"Um, er, yes," I agreed. I turned beetroot-red. **Oh, why was I such a bumbling mess around Petunia?** Was it because she was so sweet? Was it because she was so cute? Was it because she didn't seem to notice she was so sweet and cute and that I was a **BUMBLING MESS?**

I was still thinking about it as we boarded the plane for home. Petunia sat next to me. I checked my seat belt ten times, then read the air safety manual from front to back. Did I mention I hate flying? Luckily, Petunia didn't seem to notice. **Ah, what a mouse!**

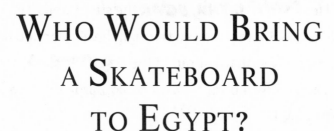

WHO WOULD BRING A SKATEBOARD TO EGYPT?

At long last, we arrived in New Mouse City. I waited for the aeroplane door to open. Then I began climbing down the stairs. But, I **TRIPPED** on something! It was pink. It was flat. It had wheels. **CHEESE NIBLETS!** Who would bring a **skateboard** to Egypt?

"Hey, watch out for my skateboard, Uncle G!" I heard Bugsy yell. Too late.

I fell **DOWN**, **DOWN**, **DOWN** the steep steps. I went into a spin. I somersaulted through the air. I landed flat on my belly with my snout in the **PAVEMENT**.

Then I wiggled my paws. I could hardly believe it. I was alive!

Two seconds later, Bugsy's skateboard landed on my head. I was out like a light.

Is Your Brain Still Working?

When I came around, I was in the New Mouse City Hospital. I was wrapped in so many **BANDAGES**, I looked just like an Egyptian mummy.

My head was **POUNDING**. I remembered the awful nightmare that had woken me. I dreamed that I was trapped in the Egyptian Mouseum and I was being chased by a **terrifying** mummy. And there was a pesky little girl who had a pink skateboard. And I tripped on the skateboard and fell down some stairs. And the pesky little girl kept calling me in a high, squeaky voice … **"Uncle, G! Uncle G!"** a high-pitched voice broke into my thoughts. Startled, I saw a face peering down at me. It was a little female mouse with black braids.

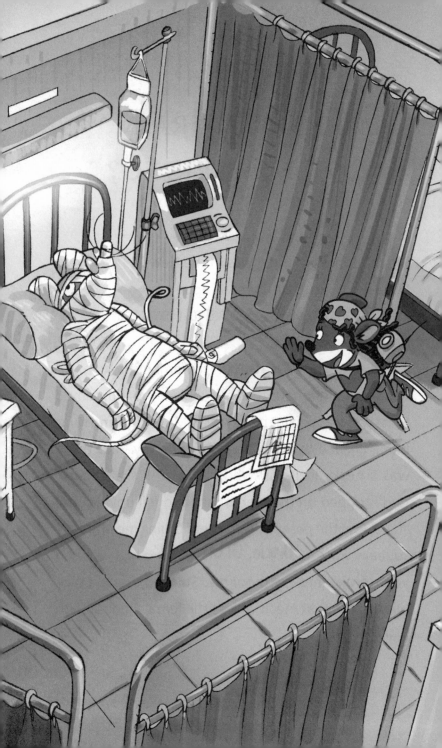

My eyes popped open wide. **"B-b-b-bugsy?"** I stammered.

"Uncle G! You're alive!" she squeaked. Then she waved her paws in front of my face. "Ok, Uncle G, let's see if your brain is still working. How many fingers do you see? Huh? How many? **How many?**" she shrieked. Then she rapped on my bandaged head. **"Hello, in there! Can you hear me?"** she yelled.

Now my head was really pounding. "Two! Two! I see two fingers!" I shouted.

"Don't talk, Uncle G. Don't even squeak! You need to rest! To relax! To eat! To sleep! And you're in **luck**. I'm here to take care of you!" she announced.

Fortunately, my nephew Benjamin arrived before I had a **HEART ATTACK**. "How are you feeling, Uncle?" he asked, patting my paw softly.

"I'm feeling fine, Benjamin," I said. What could I say? Your little friend Bugsy is a total **pain in my fur?** "I'm just sorry that I can't organise the Halloween party I promised you," I groaned.

Right then, Bugsy jumped to her paws. **"Surprise!"** she cried in an ear-piercing squeak. "Not to worry, **Uncle G**, I'm one step ahead of you. I've already organised your Halloween party. You're going to have an awesome **MUMMY PARTY!**" Benjamin nodded. "It's going to be fabumouse, Uncle!" he squeaked.

Hmm. A mummy party? To tell you the truth, I was still a little afraid of mummies. I mean, even though we discovered the MVMMY WITH NO NAME wasn't alive, the whole idea still made my fur stand on end.

Bugsy was going on and on about her party plans. It seemed she had baked cookies shaped like mummies, made up a **CREEPY** mummy dance, and sent the guests invitations in the shape of a sarcophagus.

"And you won't believe **HOW MANY RODENTS** are coming, Uncle G," Bugsy continued. "I invited all your friends, all your neighbours, everyone at The Rodent's Gazette and at the Egyptian Mouseum, the mailmouse, the bin mouse, the sewer rat, and loads of other perfect strangers I met on the street. Your house is going to be **PACKED!**"

Perfect strangers? Packed? Can you guess what happened next? Yes. I fainted. Fortunately, **I was already lying in bed.**

A Party to Remumber

I was released from the hospital on the day of the party. When I arrived home, I saw that there were **GIANT** papier-mâché columns all around the living room and everyone was dressed in ancient Egyptian costumes. Bugsy introduced me to her baby brother **Trouble** – the name says it all. Her cousin **ZAK**, on the other paw, was very funny. He got along with my young assistant, Pinky Pick. Before long, the two were laughing and telling silly MUMMY JOKES ...

Trouble

ZAK

I have to admit, the party was truly fabumouse.

ZAK AND PINKY'S
MUMMY JOKES

What did the baby mummy say when he got lost at the supermarket?

I want my mummy!

What did the mummy say when she landed on the moon?

One small step for mummy, one giant leap for mummykind!

Why did the mummy go to the hospital?

He had a mummyache.

What do you call a mummy who plays a guitar?

A strummy mummy!

Bugsy taught all of the guests a game she called the **EGYPTIAN CONNIPTION**. And everyone munched on mummy cookies and bobbed for apples floating in a plastic sarcophagus.

The guests had a **SUPER** time. And I have to say, I was feeling a little less creeped out by the whole mummy thing. **After all, it's not every day that you get to meet a Mummy with No Name ...**

HOW TO ORGANISE A
CHILLING
MVMMY
PARTY

MVMMY CHAIN

WHAT YOU NEED:

- Brown paper
- Pencil
- Round-tipped scissors
- Sticky tape

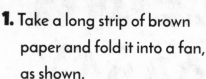

1. Take a long strip of brown paper and fold it into a fan, as shown.

2. Draw the form of a mummy on the top sheet and cut around the figure with the round-tipped scissors.

3. Open the mummy chain and hang it on the walls of the party room with sticky tape.

MUMMIFIED TABLE

WHAT YOU NEED:

- Toilet paper
- White tissue paper
- Brown construction paper
- Round-tipped scissors
- Glue

1. Wrap the table's and chairs' legs with toilet paper in such a way that they appear mummified.

2. Cover the entire table with white tissue paper.

3. On brown construction paper, draw lots of scarabs and then cut them out with the round-tipped scissors. You may draw or trace the scarabs from the drawing on this page.

4. Glue the scarabs around the border of the entire tissue-paper tablecloth as shown.

ABOUT THE AUTHOR

Born in New Mouse City, Mouse Island, GERONIMO STILTON is Rattus Emeritus of Mousomorphic Literature and of Neo-Ratonic Comparative Philosophy. For the past twenty years, he has been running The Rodent's Gazette, New Mouse City's most widely read daily newspaper.

Stilton was awarded the Ratitzer Prize for his scoops on *The Curse of the Cheese Pyramid* and *The Search for Sunken Treasure*. He has also received the Andersen Prize

for Personality of the Year. His works have been published all over the globe.

In his spare time, Mr. Stilton collects antique cheese rinds and plays golf. But what he most enjoys is telling stories to his nephew Benjamin.

THE RODENT'S GAZETTE

1. Main entrance
2. Printing presses (where everything is printed)
3. Accounts department
4. Editorial room (where editors, illustrators, and designers work)
5. Geronimo Stilton's office
6. Geronimo's botanical garden

MAP OF NeW MOUSE CITY

MAP OF MOUSE ISLAND

1. Big Ice Lake
2. Frozen Fur Peak
3. Slipperyslopes Glacier
4. Coldcreeps Peak
5. Ratzikistan
6. Transratania
7. Mount Vamp
8. Roastedrat Volcano
9. Brimstone Lake
10. Poopedcat Pass
11. Stinko Peak
12. Dark Forest
13. Vain Vampires Valley
14. Goosebumps Gorge
15. The Shadow Line Pass
16. Penny-Pincher Castle
17. Nature Reserve Park
18. Las Ratayas Marinas
19. Fossil Forest
20. Lake Lake
21. Lake Lakelake
22. Lake Lakelakelake
23. Cheddar Crag
24. Cannycat Castle
25. Valley of the Giant Sequoia
26. Cheddar Springs
27. Sulphurous Swamp
28. Old Reliable Geyser
29. Vole Vale
30. Ravingrat Ravine
31. Gnat Marshes
32. Munster Highlands
33. Mousehara Desert
34. Oasis of the Sweaty Camel
35. Cabbagehead Hill
36. Rattytrap Jungle
37. Rio Mosquito
38. Mousefort Beach
39. San Mouscisco
40. Swissville
41. Cheddarton
42. Mouseport
43. New Mouse City
44. Pirate Ship of Cats

THE COLLECTION

HAVE YOU READ ALL OF GERONIMO'S ADVENTURES?

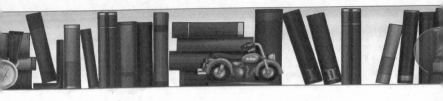

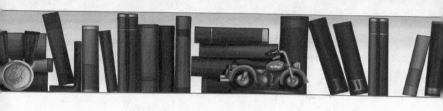

HAPPY READING!